The Pig under the Pew

by
W.G. Van de Hulst

illustrated by
Willem G. Van de Hulst, Jr.

INHERITANCE PUBLICATIONS
NEERLANDIA, ALBERTA, CANADA
PELLA, IOWA, U.S.A.

Library and Archives Canada Cataloguing in Publication

Hulst, W. G. van de (Willem Gerrit), 1879-1963
[Van de boze koster. English]
      The pig under the pew / by W.G. Van de Hulst ; illustrated
by Willem G. Van de Hulst, Jr. ; [translated by Harry der Nederlanden].
(Stories children love ; 10)
Translation of: Van de boze koster.
Originally published: St. Catharines, Ontario : Paideia Press, 1978.
ISBN 978-1-928136-10-1 (pbk.)
      I. Hulst, Willem G. van de (Willem Gerrit), 1917-, illustrator
II. Nederlanden, Harry der, translator III. Title. IV. Title: Van de boze
koster. English V. Series: Hulst, W. G. van de (Willem Gerrit), 1879-1963
Stories children love ; 10
PZ7.H873985Pig 2014   j839.313'62   C2014-903603-5

Library of Congress Cataloging-in-Publication Data

Hulst, W. G. van de (Willem Gerrit), 1879-1963.
[Van de boze koster. English]
The pig under the pew / by W.G. Van de Hulst ; illustrated by Willem G. Van de Hulst, Jr. ;
edited by Paulina Janssen.
pages cm. — (Stories children love ; #10)
"Originally published in Dutch as Van de boze koster. Original translations done by Miss J.
Blom and Harry der Nederlanden for Woudstra's Bookhouse, Edmonton-Alta-Canada &
Paideia Press, St. Catharines-Ontario-Canada."
Summary: Tim, Andy, and Ricky unintentionally anger the church's caretaker, then while
they are trying to help Lucy, the preacher's daughter, they accidentally let loose a pig
that heads into the church while the children try to catch him.
ISBN 978-1-928136-10-1
[1. Behavior—Fiction. 2. Pigs—Fiction. 3. Lost and found possessions—Fiction.] I.
Hulst, Willem G. van de (Willem Gerrit), 1917- illustrator. II. Title.
PZ7.H887Pig 2014   [E]—dc23   2014017988

Originally published in Dutch as *Van de boze koster*
Cover painting and illustrations by Willem G. Van de Hulst, Jr.
Original translations done by Miss J. Blom and Harry der Nederlanden for
Woudstra's Bookhouse, Edmonton-Alta-Canada & Paideia Press,
St. Catharines-Ontario-Canada.
The publisher expresses his appreciation to John Hultink of Paideia Press for
his generous permission to use his translation (ISBN 0-88815-510-7).

Edited by Paulina Janssen

ISBN 978-1-928136-10-1

Published simultaneously in U.S.A. by Inheritance Publications
Box 366, Pella, Iowa 50219

Printed in Canada

Contents

1. The Little Old Lady

It was very quiet along the road.
The old apple tree was covered with
thousands of blossoms: red and white,
red and white. Beside the old apple tree
stood a little old house.
Out of the little old house came a little old lady.
She had kind old eyes, but they were looking
sad.
"Oh, dear!" she said. "Oh, dear!"

She had finished washing the dishes. She had
scrubbed her old, iron pot until it shone. But it
was still wet.

She carried the iron pot to the other side of the road and put it down in the grass. The sun was shining brightly. The pot would soon dry in the sun.

The old iron pot had three short legs. It was black on the outside, but shiny on the inside. When the sun shone into it, it shone like silver.

The little old lady turned around and went back into her little old house.
"Oh, dear!" she said. "Oh, dear!"

2. The Angry Caretaker

In the little old house also lived a little old man. He was the caretaker of the church. He kept the key to the church and saw to it that the church was always neat and clean. He was very proud of the job he did. Every Sunday he rang the church bell in the steeple. The bell called all the people to church.

Listen!
What do you hear?
Was that coming from the little house?
Who was grumbling so loudly?
Oh, listen! It was the caretaker.
He grumbled at his wife,
but she had not done
anything. He was angry
because he had lost his
glasses. Now he could
not see if the pews were
dusty. And the next day
was Sunday.

So he grumbled and grumbled.

He was angry at everyone; he was very angry.

He stomped outside.

He had looked all through the house.

He decided to look along the road. He looked in the grass. He was so angry, he kicked the iron pot over.

His cap brushed the pretty blossoms of the apple tree. They fluttered down: red and white, red and white. But he was so angry, he did not care.

He looked in the orchard. Stooping, he looked in the tall grass. He grumbled and grumbled.

It was very quiet along the road.

But the sun could no longer shine into

the iron pot. It lay in the grass, its three legs sticking up in the air. The sun now shone on its black bottom.

3. The Three Little Boys

Down the road came three little boys: Tim and Andy and Ricky. They were brothers. Ricky was in the lead.

Ricky's socks sagged. Ricky's cap sat crooked. And he carried a big stick.

They saw the iron pot . . . the black pot, lying upside down in the green grass.

Ricky hit it with his stick. Bong! went the pot.

The boys laughed. Tim said, "I know! Let's cook potatoes!"

Andy did not like the idea. "We may not!" he said.

"Why not?" said Tim. "It's just an old pot. It doesn't belong to anyone. Someone threw it away. It's all right." He turned the pot right side up.

Ricky shouted, "I've got a potato!" Bong! He threw a big rock into the iron pot.

"Yes, yes!" shouted the boys. "Lots of potatoes, yes, yes!"

They started to look for more big rocks. They set the iron pot in the middle of the road and they stirred in it with the big stick. That was the spoon. They squatted down around it and made loud sizzling noises, "Ssss! Ssss!" The potatoes were cooking.

Vrrrooommm! Beep-beep!
Oh, oh! What was that? What was that?
A car came down the road. Beep-beep!
The little, happy boys jumped with fright.

They ran. They scattered.

The iron pot was left in the middle of the road. On top of it lay the big stick. That was the spoon.

Beep-beep!

The car roared by. It rode right over the iron pot. Clankity-clank! Clankity-clank! went the pot. All the cooked potatoes scattered over the road.

And the poor pot? It flew through the air and landed in the hedge.

But behind the hedge . . .

Oh, look! Look! Behind the hedge stood the caretaker. He had seen everything.

"My pot! My iron pot!" he shouted. He ran after the boys on his slippers. They went slip-slop, slip-slop across the road. He ran as fast as he could. He shook his fist at the boys. He was angry, very angry. "My pot! My iron pot!"

He tried to catch the boys — all three of them. He shouted, "You rascals! If I ever catch you, I'll lock you in my pigpen — all three of you!" He was so angry, his face was red and his eyes bulged. But he could not catch the boys. They were running much too fast.

Again he shouted, "You rascals! If I ever catch you, I'll lock you in my pigpen — all three of you!"

Then he walked back to his little old house. He took the iron pot along with him. It was dirty on the outside and filled with sand on the inside, but it wasn't broken.

The three boys ran a long, long way. Andy cried. He was frightened by the angry caretaker.

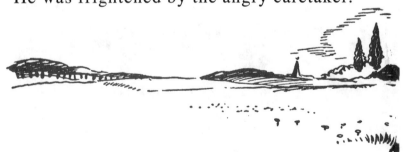

"It was your fault. It was your fault!" he sobbed.
But Tim said, "I didn't know it was his pot.
Come on, let's go play somewhere else."
Ricky tagged along behind. His socks sagged.
And his cap sat crooked on his head.

4. Lucy

Lucy was picking flowers. She wore a
pretty necklace of red and yellow beads
around her neck. When she stooped, the
beads dangled in the tall
grass.
Do you know who Lucy
was? Lucy was the
preacher's little girl. She
lived in the big house
beside the church. Her

hair was blonde and curly and she wore a pretty, blue dress.

She walked down the quiet little lane not far from home. Mother had told her she could go a little way down the lane.

Along the lane was a big gate. Behind the gate was a big meadow. It belonged to the caretaker. Lucy peeked through the boards of the gate. In the meadow there were beautiful flowers, lots and lots of them. She climbed on the gate. Her pretty beads tinkled against the boards.

Suddenly the gate swung open a little way, just a crack.

At first it scared Lucy a little. But then her eyes sparkled with delight. Quickly she climbed back down. Squeezing through the crack, she sneaked into the meadow —

very slowly, very carefully.

There were such beautiful flowers in the meadow! Lots and lots of them.
Lucy only had eyes for the flowers. Slowly she went farther and farther into the meadow. She picked more and more flowers: white flowers, yellow flowers, and blue flowers.
Oh, that foolish Lucy! Foolish Lucy!

5. Swish, Swish, Swish

Very faintly something far out in the meadow went, "Oink, oink!"
But Lucy did not hear it. She was too busy picking flowers.

"Oink, oink, oink!"
And seven pink snouts stuck up out of the grass.
And seven pairs of tiny eyes peered at the little girl.
And seven little tails curled with delight.
But Lucy did not see them. Oh, no.

15

Swish, swish, swish went the grass. And seven little pigs ran toward her as fast as they could. Their little pink snouts stuck up out of the grass. They thought the little girl had come to feed them.

Their curly tails twitched up and down in delight. Their tails looked like corkscrews.

Swish, swish, swish went the grass.

Suddenly Lucy saw them. She froze in fright.

"Mother, Mother!" she screamed. "Mother, oh, Mother!"

But Mother did not hear her. Mother was too far away. And the seven little pigs ran even faster.

"No, no, no! Go away, you ugly beasts!"

Lucy closed her eyes in fright. She held out her hands as if to stop the little pigs, her hands that were filled with flowers.

"No, no, no!" she sobbed. "Go away!"

But the seven little pigs frisked around her in a little circle. Poor Lucy . . . she was surrounded.

"Oink, oink! Oink, oink!"

They held up their little snouts. They sniffed at Lucy's dress. They sniffed at Lucy's legs. They sniffed at her pretty beads.

One of the little piglets jumped up and tried to take a bite of Lucy's flowers. Another little piglet darted between her legs. And still another one put his forepaws up against the front of Lucy's dress.

"Oink, oink! Oink, oink, oink!"

Lucy was terrified.

Tears ran down her cheeks. She tried to run away, but those horrible pigs came after her. Finally she did not even dare move.

Lucy was terrified. Those horrible, ugly beasts! She did not know what to do.

"Mother! Mother!" she screamed.

But Mother did not hear her. She was too far away.

"Oink, oink, oink!" the little pigs went around her. "Oink, oink, oink!"

Poor Lucy! Who would help her?

6. The Brave Boys

The gate squeaked.
A little boy peeked around the corner of the gate.
His socks sagged and his cap sat crooked. He saw poor Lucy in the meadow. The pigs frightened him too. Bang! Quickly he pulled the gate shut.

But then . . . then another boy ran down the lane. And another. They also heard Lucy's cries. They heard her scream.
It frightened them. Fearfully, the three boys peered through the gate.

But Tim became angry at what he saw. He became angry at those mean pigs. And Tim was a brave boy.
He pushed the gate open. He shouted, "Shoo! Shoo! You mean little pigs. I'll tell the preacher!" And he walked right out into the meadow.

Andy looked very frightened. But he was a brave boy too. He, too, walked into the meadow, but very carefully and only a little way.

And Ricky? Oh, Ricky was the bravest of all. He quickly climbed up on the gate and at the top of his voice he shouted, "Shoo! Shoo! Mean pigs! I'll tell the preacher on you!"

The little pigs were frightened by all the noise. Swish, swish, swish! They ran away through the tall grass.

But soon they stopped. Boldly they stuck their little snouts up in the air. "Oink, oink, oink!"

Tim quickly grabbed Lucy by the hand. "Come on, Lucy. Hurry! I'll help you."

Together they ran toward the gate. Andy ran ahead of them to show them the way. And Ricky, standing on the gate, shouted, "Come on. I'll help you!"

And the seven little pigs . . . ran after them. Swish, swish, swish!

"Run! Run for the gate! Hurry, through the crack!"

Oh, oh! Look, Lucy's necklace caught on the post. The pretty necklace snapped and all the beads fell into the grass: red and yellow, red and yellow. Poor Lucy!

But Tim and Andy and Ricky were brave boys. Tim stopped and took off his wooden shoe. Angrily he waved it at the little pigs. He shouted, "Come on, I dare you! I dare you, you mean pigs! Ha, you're afraid!"

Ricky took off his wooden shoe too. From behind the gate he shouted, "You're afraid! You're afraid!"

Andy was on his hands and knees looking for the beads. And so was Lucy. Big tears rolled down her cheeks. Poor Lucy!

Together they walked back down the lane. Ricky was still holding his wooden shoe. He kept looking back and shouting, "You're afraid! You're afraid!"

The little pigs wandered back into the meadow. Except for one little pig. He came back to the gate.

The gate was still standing open, just a crack. The little rascal stuck his snout around the corner. His tail curled in delight.
And no one saw him.

7. A Beautiful Spot

Near the church lay a beautiful spot. The sun shone against the stone wall. The grass was very tall and big pieces of stone lay in the grass. They had fallen off the church a long time ago. They had been there for almost one hundred years. They were so old, they were green and yellow and gold.
That was the spot Tim, Andy, Ricky, and Lucy were headed for. Lucy walked in the middle. Tim

held one of her hands and Andy the other. They were very kind to her. They felt sorry for her. Ricky tagged along behind, hobbling along on one stocking foot. He was the bravest one of all.

They sat down to string the beads back on the necklace. They laid them all on one of the old stones. The sun shone down on them and made them sparkle: red and yellow and gold.
Tim pushed the string through the beads. Lucy slid the beads down the string. Andy watched the other beads so they wouldn't roll off the stone.
And Ricky? Ricky sat in the tall grass. He had a hole in one of his socks. His toe was peeking through. Ricky laughed. He pulled his big toe and said, "This little pig went to market . . ." Then he tried to pull out the other piggies.

Suddenly . . . swish, swish!
A little pig ran by. It ran through the tall grass and right over Ricky's foot.
Ricky yelped in fright. He tumbled over backwards, his legs in the air.
Startled, Tim snapped the string of beads.

Lucy screamed, "Mother! Mother!"
And Andy quickly threw himself on the pretty
beads. He was afraid the pig might scatter them.
The little pig, the naughty little rascal, ran on.
His little corkscrew curled in delight.
The little rascal had snuck through the gate.
"Oink, oink, oink!"

8. Catch Him!

Where was the little pig going?
No one knew.

Peeking around the church wall, the children watched him go.
Tim looked frightened.
He was not afraid of the little pig.
He was afraid of the little pig's owner.
It belonged to the caretaker. What if the caretaker found out?
They had left the gate open. So it was their fault!
What if the caretaker found out?

"Who's coming with me?" asked Tim, very bravely. "I'm going to catch him. Who's coming?"
Catch him? Catch one of those ugly little beasts?
Lucy shuddered.
Andy looked frightened. But not Ricky. He said, "Let's catch him. Ugly pig!" He held up both of his wooden shoes in his hands.

Oh, look! The little pig was sniffing along the church wall. Not far in front of him was a small door. It stood open, just a crack. And what do you think the little rascal did?

He pushed his little snout through the crack. The door opened farther.

Then he pushed his whole head into the church.

Then his whole body.

Only his curly tail still showed.

Oh, oh, the children were shocked.

"He may not go in there!" cried Lucy.

"Pigs aren't allowed in the church!"

"No, no piggy!" shouted Ricky. "You may not!"

"Catch him! Catch him!"

Tim ran after the little pig. He tried to grab him by his curly tail. Missed! He just missed!

The curly tail popped inside the church too. Now the whole pig was in the church. And that was not allowed. A pig in the church — that was terrible!

Tim and Andy and Ricky and even Lucy carefully tiptoed to the door and peeked inside. Ricky knelt on the steps to see.

Andy quickly put all the pretty beads into his pocket. He put them deep into the corner so they wouldn't fall out. He was afraid they might get lost.

Very softly Tim whispered, "Are you going to come into the church with me? We have to chase that pig back out."

"Yes," whispered Andy, nodding. "We have to!" And Ricky nodded too.

But Lucy did not dare. "No, I'm not going in there with that ugly beast. I'm scared!" She looked as if she was ready to cry.

"Don't be scared, Lucy. Come on. Just stay behind me. I'll grab him."

Very carefully they stole inside the partly open door — first Tim, then Andy, then Lucy, and last of all Ricky. They walked very, very quietly. The boys took off their wooden shoes. They knew that they weren't allowed in the church on

their wooden shoes. The shoes stayed behind by the door — all six of them.

"Where did the naughty little pig go?"

Down the quiet lane came an old man. But the children did not see him come.

The old man looked at the ground and he grumbled to himself. He was so angry, there were three deep wrinkles in his forehead.

He saw that the gate to the meadow was standing open a little and he became even angrier. He kicked it shut.

He grumbled, "My glasses . . . Where are my glasses?"

He looked everywhere: in the lane, in the grass, under the bushes.

And then — then he looked through the bushes . . . and suddenly he saw a little pig run around the church. And four little children chasing it.

He saw the little pig slip into his clean church.

And he saw the children steal in after it. And tomorrow was Sunday! He stomped in anger. "Those rascals! Those rowdy rascals! I'll teach them! I'll teach them!"

Slip, slop! Slip, slop!

He hurried down the lane.

He clenched both fists.

Then he, too, slipped inside the church door.

Oh, oh, what would happen now?

9. Under the Pews

Very carefully the boys tiptoed through the church. They knew they were not allowed to make noise in the church.

Lucy wore her shoes. They went, tip-tap, tip-tap, on the floor. She was scared of the little pig.

But Tim said, "Just stay behind me. I'm not scared."

"I'm not scared!" said Ricky. But he quickly hid behind Lucy. That was how brave he was.

Suddenly Andy cried, "I see him! I see him! Over there!"

Sure enough. There sat the little pig — on the steps of the pulpit. He stuck his little snout up in the air. When he saw the children, he quickly hopped down and ran off through the church. His little feet slipped on the slippery stone floor. The floor was very clean, because tomorrow was Sunday.

The little pig ran under the pulpit and under the pews. He ran this way and that way. He ran everywhere. And the children ran after him.

Tim almost had him by the tail. He just missed.

But then . . . the little side door of the church squeaked, but none of the children heard it. And then . . . the angry caretaker stumbled over the

wooden shoes by the door, but none of the children heard that either.

"Rascals! Rascals!"

Oh, then!
All of a sudden the children saw the old man. He picked up the little wooden shoes — all six of them. And he put them into his coat pockets. He grumbled and grumbled.
Oh, the poor children.
They trembled with fear.
They did not know what to do.
They huddled close together.

They held onto one another in fright.

Tim thought, "I'll tell him we're trying to catch the pig . . . Because pigs aren't allowed in the church . . . And then the caretaker won't be angry at us."

But Tim also thought, "I'm afraid. We left the gate open. So it's our fault. And we put the caretaker's iron pot on the road. No, I'm afraid to talk to him. What if he grabs me! "

There came the angry old man. He did not see the children.

They hid beside a high pew. It had a little door in the side.

"Come on. Follow me," whispered Tim.

On his hands and knees, he crawled into the pew. Andy quickly followed him. So did Lucy. Her bare knees got bruised on the hard stone floor. But she was so scared, she hardly felt it. Ricky tagged along behind them. His socks sagged and his cap sat crooked on his head. They all hid in the high pew and quietly closed the little door.

Slip, slop! Slip, slop!

Oh, oh, there came the caretaker, shuffling along

on his big slippers. He grumbled and grumbled.
He saw the little pig. But where were those
rascals, those rowdy little
rascals? He did not see any
sign of them. Where could
they have gone?
He had to find them! And
when he did, he would lock
them all up in the pigpen.
Slip, slop! Slip, slop!

10. Oh, No!

Slip, slop!
The caretaker shuffled past the pew.
Slip, slop!
He did not see the frightened children hiding inside.
The pew was too high.
Slip, slop! Slip, slop!
He shuffled through the church.
He grumbled and grumbled.

The children sat very still. They listened to his footsteps. Their hearts pounded.
Suddenly, Ricky felt something hard under him. He picked it up. "Oh, look!" he cried.
"Shhh! Quiet, Ricky!"
"Look!" he cried again. "I found . . ."
"Shhh! If the caretaker hears you!"
But Ricky was not thinking about the caretaker. All he could think of was the wonderful thing he had found. It was black and rather flat and it rattled when he shook it.
"But look!" he cried even louder. "I found . . ."
"Shhh! Quiet!"

Oh, no.
There came the caretaker again. He had heard them!

He growled, "Just wait till I catch you, you rascals. I'll lock you up in my pigpen."

"Hurry, hurry! Follow me!" hissed Tim. Tim was the oldest. He was also the smartest. "Hurry!" He crawled to the other end of the pew. There was another little door at that end. The others all crawled along behind him.

Lucy whimpered, "Mother! Mother!"

Ricky clutched the wonderful thing he had found tightly in his hand.

At the other end of the pew, they darted back into the church. Ricky tripped, scraping his knee. He hardly felt it. He was too worried about losing the black treasure in his hand.

"Stop! Stop, you little rascals!" the caretaker shouted angrily.

But they did not stop. They were much too frightened. They ran to the other end of the church. The caretaker lurched along after them. He did not see that the little girl running away from him was the preacher's little girl. He could not see the children very well. He had lost his glasses.

He thought he was chasing a group of naughty children — rowdy rascals. "I'll teach you! I'll teach you!" he growled.

And no one thought about the little pig anymore.
"Mother! Mother!" cried Lucy. "Oh, Mother!"
But suddenly her voice did not sound frightened anymore.

Why?

In the back of the church she saw a door. She knew that door. It led into a big yard. That was her yard. She ran to the door. "Mother! Mother!" She pushed at it with her hands and with her whole body.

Tim pushed too.

And so did Andy.

Ricky did too. But he did not let go of the black treasure he had found.

"Hurry! Hurry! The caretaker is coming. Hurry!"

11. Crash!

The preacher sat in his study reading the Bible and many other big books. The next day was Sunday.

On Sunday the church bell would ring and all the people would come to church. Then the preacher would tell them about God and about the Lord Jesus who lives in Heaven and who sees everything. The Bible told the preacher what to say, because it is God's book.

The preacher had been reading and thinking for a long time. It was very quiet in the study.

The sun shone through the big window. The apple trees in the yard were covered with thousands of blossoms: red and white, red and white.

The preacher was thinking about the text. He was not thinking about little children playing out in the sunshine. And he was not thinking about little children who went where they were not supposed to.

Listen!
What was that?
Did he hear something inside the church? The

church was always quiet during the week. What was going on?

Listen!
He heard it again.
He looked out the window.

He could see the back door of the church. It was the door he always used to go into the church. It was closed now.

Listen!
He was sure he heard something. Someone was shouting inside the church, on the other side of the door. The preacher stared. What was going on?

Crash! Suddenly the door burst open.

The preacher jumped up, startled. He could hardly believe his eyes. And then a tangle of children tumbled out into the yard. They tumbled over each other onto the path. One of them was Lucy, his own little girl. They all shouted and screamed.
Right behind them a little pig ran out of the church. It jumped over the tangle of children. And right behind the pig came the caretaker. He made a grab for the pig, but he just missed. As he stooped, a whole group of little wooden shoes spilled out of his coat pockets. He stood up and shook his fist, "You rascals! You rowdy little rascals!"

The preacher was shocked at first. But then he began to laugh. He laughed out loud.

But he had no idea what was going on. What was it all about?

His little girl, and three little boys, and a pig, and wooden shoes, and the caretaker? And they had all burst out of the church at the same time! No, he had no idea what was going on. But it sure looked funny. He laughed and laughed.

He hurried to the kitchen. "Dear! Dear, come and see what's happening in the back yard. Ha-ha-ha!"

Lucy's mother was just making supper. She asked, "Why? What's going on? What's so funny?"

"Ha-ha-ha! Come and see!"

Together they hurried into the back yard. Mother carried the soup ladle in her hand.

12. My Glasses!

Lucy ran toward them, holding out her arms.
"Mother! Mother!" she sobbed.
Her dress was dirty, her hands were dirty, and her face was dirty.
"Lucy, how did you get so dirty? What happened? What's the matter?"
But all Lucy said was, "Mother! Mother!" She was so upset. But she was also happy.
Tim and Andy quickly grabbed their wooden shoes. They crawled against the wall with them. They were very bashful.
But not Ricky. He sat in the grass. His cap on his head sat crooked. He tried to open the flat little box.
The caretaker stood in the door, shaking his head. He was still angry. "Those rascals!" he said to the preacher. "Those rowdy little rascals!" And he told the preacher everything: about the iron pot, about the gate, about the little pig, and about the church. "I had no idea Lucy was with them. I can't see too well. I lost my glasses."
Suddenly Ricky cried, "Look! Isn't it pretty? I found it!"

They all looked at Ricky. They gathered around him. What had he found?

Look! He opened the black thing he had found. The black thing was a case. Out of it Ricky pulled a pair of glasses.

They were the caretaker's glasses. The caretaker saw them.

"My glasses! My glasses!" Suddenly he was no longer angry. He was smiling. "You found my glasses!"

He lifted Ricky up and said, "You're not a little rascal. You're a good little boy! You found my glasses for me. Yes, you're a good boy!

"Come along with me. I have a little treat for you. I'm not angry anymore. All of you come along."

The preacher laughed. "What about the little pig?" he asked. "Can he come along too?"

The little pig! They had all forgotten about the little pig. Together they went after him. The naughty little rascal squealed in fright!

"Oink, oink! Oink, oink, oink!"

But he was trapped in the back yard. He ran between the preacher's legs and tried to get back into the church. But Mother blocked his way with the soup ladle. Tim grabbed him by the tail.

"Oink, oink, oink!"

He was caught.

The caretaker laughed. He put his glasses on. His smile grew even wider. He laughed. "Come on, you little rascals. Come along with me!"

13. Tomorrow is Sunday

And there they went!
The old caretaker led the way. He carried the little pig under his arm. His glasses were on his nose. And he wore a big smile.
Tim and Andy and Lucy walked behind him. Last of all came Ricky. His socks sagged and his cap sat crooked.
First they brought the little pig back to the meadow. Then they went to the little old lady in the little old house beside the apple tree.
She was standing in the doorway. She looked

sad. Her iron pot was again standing in the grass. She had washed it again. It was black on the outside and shiny on the inside. When the sun shone into it, it shone like silver.

The little old lady saw them coming down the road. Her eyes widened in surprise. She looked and looked. Then she saw the glasses on the old man's nose. She clapped her hands in delight. Suddenly her sadness was gone.

"Did you find your glasses? Dear, dear! I was so worried! But what are you doing with all these little children? And where did you find your glasses?"

"I found them!" Ricky said proudly. "I found them!"

"You, you little youngster? You found them?"

"That's right!" said the caretaker. "He found them. He found them in the church. He's a good boy, a fine boy. And he's here for a treat. I'm going to treat them all because I gave them such a scare."

Then they all followed the little old lady into the little old house. She gave each of the children a little bag with four big maple cream balls.

But Ricky got five of them.
That was only fair.

And then the children all went home.
And then evening came.

When the three brothers came home, their mother
put them all in the bathtub. She said they were
as dirty as little pigs. And tomorrow was Sunday.
Andy took off his pants.
Rick-a-tick, rick-a-tick-tick!
Oh . . . many, many round little balls rolled onto
the floor: red and yellow, red and yellow. He
blushed.
"Those are Lucy's!" He had forgotten all about
the pretty beads.
Mother laughed and said, "Don't worry. She can
do without them until tomorrow. You can give
them back to her in the morning. You can wait
for her after church.
"But now into the tub with you — all three of
you. Tomorrow is Sunday."

Night came.
And in the middle of the night Andy woke up.
He looked beside his bed. Beside his bed stood

a chair. The moonlight fell on a little box standing on the chair. And in that box . . .

Andy picked it up and shook it a little. It rattled. He opened it a little and peeked inside. Red and yellow, red and yellow.
Then he put it back on the chair and crawled back under the covers.
"Tomorrow!" he mumbled. "Won't Lucy be happy!"

Titles in this series: